January

February

March

April

May

June

July

August

September

BEGINNER BOOKS   A Division of Random House, Inc.

October

November

December

Please Try
to Remember
the FIRST of
OCTEMBER!

OCTEMBER

by Theo. LeSieg
Illustrated by Art Cumings

Copyright © 1977 by Dr. Seuss and A. S. Geisel. Illustrations Copyright © 1977 by Random House, Inc. All rights reserved under International and Pan-American Copyright Conventions. Published in the United States by Random House, Inc., New York, and simultaneously in Canada by Random House of Canada Limited, Toronto. *Library of Congress Cataloging in Publication Data:* Seuss, Dr. Please try to remember the first of Octember! "B 63." SUMMARY: Every wish is fulfilled on the First of Octember. [1. Wishes—Fiction. 2. Stories in rhyme] I. Cumings, Art. II. Title. PZ8.3.G276Pl [E] 77-4504 ISBN 0-394-83563-8 ISBN 0-394-93563-2 lib. bdg. Manufactured in the United States of America.

F G H   9012

Everyone wants
a big green kangaroo.

Maybe, perhaps,
you would like
to have TWO.

I want you to have them.
I'll buy them for you . . .

. . . if you'll wait
till the First of October.

Everyone wants
a new skateboard TV.
Some people want two.
And some people want three.

Perhaps you want four?

Well, that's O.K. with me . . .

. . . if you'll wait

till the First of Octember.

Just say what you want.

You want pickles on trees?

Want to swing
through the air
on a flying trapeze?

Just say what you want,
and whatever you say,
you'll get
on October the First.

When October comes round,
you can play a hot tune
on your very expensive
new Jook-a-ma-Zoon!

I wish you could play it

in May or in June.

But May is too early.

And June is too soon.

When October gets here,
no work! And no school!

We'll build you a playhouse!
We'll build you a pool!
We would build them
right now,
but right now
is too cool.

And we'll buy you
a wonderful
Jeep-a-Fly kite!

We will!
If you'll wait
till the month is just right.

Octember's the best
because March is too dusty.
And April won't do
because April's too gusty.

What <u>more</u> do you want?

Do you and your dog
want more time to relax? . . .
Less time on your feet
and more time on your backs? . . .
More time in the air
and less time on the ground? . . .

You'll get it
as soon as
October comes round.

Want to take a great trip?
Well, I know a great ship!

It sails
to Alaska,
Nebraska and Sweden,
making stops
in Ga-Dopps
and the Garden of Eden.

And it sails on the First of Octember!

What <u>else</u> do you want?

Want to play a new sport?

In Octember
we'll build you
a Hock-Zocker court!

You'll get all that you want.

You just write out your list.

<u>Everyone</u> has an October First list.

Write slowly now!
Don't break your wrist.

Then one of these days
the October First van
will drive up to your house
just as fast as it can.

Whatever you want,
you will get in big bags,
and boxes and crates
with your name on the tags.

You'll have
rockets to shoot.

You'll have
bombs you can burst . . .

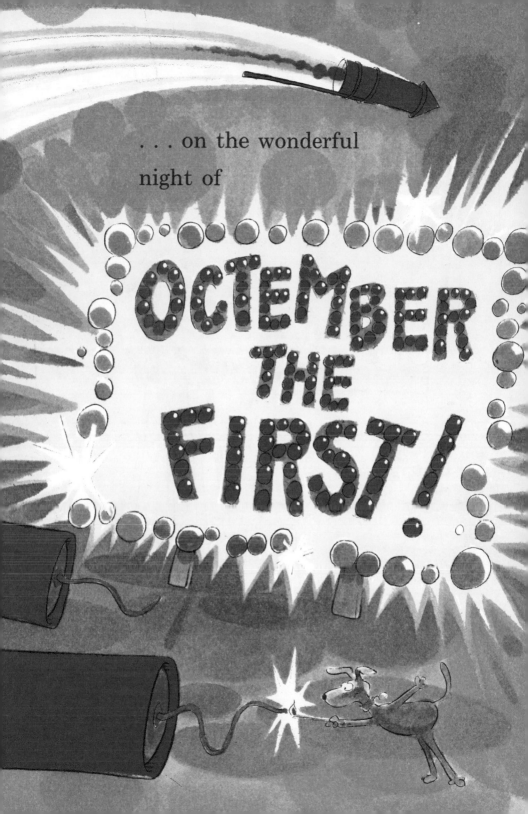

. . . on the wonderful
night of

OCTEMBER
THE
FIRST!

On the First of October
you'll stay up all night,
drinking 66 six-packs
of Doodle Delight.

Whatever
you ask for,
I want
you to get.

But October—

I'm sorry—

just isn't <u>here</u> yet.

SO . . .

Be sure
to be here.
Be sure you're in town
on Octember the First . . .

. . . when
the
money
comes
down!

It doesn't
come down much
in March
or November—
or even September . . .

. . . or in August,

October,

July

or December.

But
EVERYTHING'S
YOURS . . .

. . . on the First
of Octember!

On the First
of October?

Thank <u>you</u>!
I'll remember.

THEO. LESIEG is almost as well known to beginning readers as his mentor, Dr. Seuss. They both write wonderful stories that delight and entertain millions of children the world over. But, whereas Dr. Seuss also illustrates the stories he writes, Theo. LeSieg likes to have someone else draw the pictures for his books. In this particular case he's chosen ...

ART CUMINGS, who has been a cartoonist and illustrator for major magazines for many years. When his three sons were youngsters, Mr. Cumings decided to start illustrating books for children. This is his first Beginner Book, an assignment he especially enjoyed since it gave him the opportunity to illustrate a book by one of his favorite writers. Mr. and Mrs. Cumings live in Douglaston, New York.